Babies Can Sleep ANYWHERE

written by
LISA WHEELER

illustrated by
CAROLINA BÚZIO

Abrams Appleseed · New York

Puppy dogs sleep in a pile on a rug.
Kitty cats snooze in a chair.

A turtle tucks into his shell nice and snug.

But babies can
sleep anywhere.

Sloth stretches out in a
moss-covered tree.

Cougars curl up in a lair.

Whales settle down in
the deepest blue sea.

But babies can sleep anywhere.

Bats take a nap in a
cave upside down.

Hay is a bed for a mare.

Wolves cuddle up
in a den 'neath
the ground.

But babies can
sleep anywhere.

Squirrel's nutty nest
is all littered with twigs.

Little goats rest in a pair.

Mole makes
his bed in a hole
that he digs.

But babies can
sleep anywhere.

Skunk shuts her eyes
in a hollowed-out log.

A cave is a cot
for a bear.

Moose takes a snooze in a cranberry bog.

But babies can sleep anywhere.

In backpacks,
on knees,

in ones, twos,
and threes,

on farms or in towns, (sometimes upside down!),
on a bike, in a chair, or slumped on the stair,
sweet babies can sleep anywhere!

To the Dewitt, Saunders, and Wheeler kids, my
Yooper nieces and nephews. Love you all!
-L.W.

To my nieces, Leonor and Beatriz.
-C.B.

Cataloging-in-Publication Data has been applied for
and may be obtained from the Library of Congress.

ISBN: 978-1-4197-2536-4

Text © 2017 Lisa Wheeler
Illustrations copyright © 2017 Carolina Búzio.
Book design by Alyssa Nassner

Printed and bound in China
10 9 8 7 6 5 4 3 2 1

For bulk discount inquiries, contact specialsales@abramsbooks.com.

ABRAMS The Art of Books
115 West 18th Street, New York, NY 10011
abramsbooks.com

From GHOULIES and GHOSTIES and long leggety BEASTIES and things that go BUMP in the night, Good lord DELIVER US!

STORIES BY
AMBROSE BIERCE — LEWIS CARROLL
CHARLES DICKENS — EUGENE FIELD
KENNETH MORRIS — PHIL ROBINSON
MARY WOLLSTONECRAFT SHELLEY

RETOLD BY STEVEN ZORN

ILLUSTRATED BY JOHN BRADLEY

COURAGE
BOOKS

AN IMPRINT OF RUNNING PRESS
PHILADELPHIA • LONDON

CONTENTS

9 8 7 6 5 4 3 2 1

Digit on the right indicates the number of this printing.

Library of Congress Cataloging-in-Publication Number 93-70586

ISBN 0-7624-0407-8

Printed in China

Edited by **Gregory C. Aaron**
Design and art direction by **Alastair Campbell**
Cover illustration by **John Bradley**
John Bradley is represented by Folio, 10 Gate Street, Lincoln's Inn Fields, London WC2A 3HP

Published by Courage Books, an imprint of Running Press Book Publishers 125 South Twenty-second Street Philadelphia, Pennsylvania 19103-4399

INTRODUCTION

What are Monsters?

Are all monsters *Evil* and *Ugly*? Do they all want to *Harm* you? Fairy-tale *Dragons* breathe *Fire*, and are certainly *Monstrous*. But what about *Beautiful* dragons that *Soar* through the sky on *Jeweled* wings? Are they *Monsters*, too?

Monsters can be *Big* or *small*. They can be *Nasty* and *Scary*, or *Gentle* and *Cute*. Monsters can be *Whatever* you want them to be, Because they live only in the *Imagination*. So if you want to *Thrill* yourself with a horrible *Creature*, go ahead and *Make one up*. When you've Had your fill of *Chills*, send your *Monster* away.

In these Pages prowl *Goblins*, dragons, *Werewolves*, mad *Machines*, man-eating *Plants*, and more. This *Ghoulish* gallery will show you *Monsters* that live in *Other* people's imaginations. Some of these *Monsters* are made to *Scare* you. *Others* just want to be your *Friends*. That's the *Problem* with *Monsters* — you never know *Which* is *which*... Until it's *too late*.

So Approach with *Caution*, but be sure to have fun. *Remember* — the scariest *Monsters* are the ones you make up *Yourself*.

—STEVEN ZORN

THE WEREWOLF

BY EUGENE FIELD

MORE THAN ONE THOUSAND years ago, in the reign of Egbert the Saxon, there lived in Britain a maiden named Yseult. She was loved by all, both for her goodness and for her beauty. But though many young men sought her hand in marriage, she loved Harold only. She and Harold planned to wed.

Another young man who loved Yseult was Alfred. He was angry that Yseult showed favor to Harold. One day Alfred said to Harold: "Isn't it time for old Siegfried to come from his grave and marry Yseult?" Then he added, "Good sir, why do you turn so white when I speak your dead grandfather's name?"

Harold asked, "Why do you taunt me? What do you know about Siegfried?"

"I know what I know," replied Alfred. "My grandmother told me some tales about Siegried that I have not forgotten."

From then on, Alfred's words and bitter smile haunted Harold by day and night.

Harold's grandfather, Siegfried, had been a man of cruel violence. Legend said that a curse had rested upon him. At certain times an evil spirit had possessed Siegfried, causing him to do terrible deeds. But Siegfried had been dead for many years. There was nothing left of him but his strange spear, which had been given to him by Brunehilde, the witch. This spear never lost its brightness. Its edge could not be dulled. It hung in Harold's chamber, and it was a marvel among the weapons of that time.

But Alfred had hit the truth: the curse of old Siegfried was upon Harold. Slumbering a century, it had awakened in the blood of the grandson. Harold knew the curse was upon him, and it stood between him and Yseult.

Harold did not tell Yseult of the curse, for he feared that she would not love him if she knew. Whenever he felt the fire of the curse burning in his veins, he would say to her, "Tomorrow I hunt the wild boar in the distant forest," or, "Next week I go stag-stalking among the northern hills." Yseult trusted Harold and accepted these excuses, even though he went away often and was gone for many days.

Now in those times the country was ravaged by a werewolf—a creature feared by even the bravest men. This werewolf was by day a man, but by night a fearsome beast. The werewolf had a charmed life, and human weapons could not harm him. Wherever he attacked, he devoured people, spreading terror everywhere he roamed. The dream-readers said that the earth would not be freed from the werewolf until a man volunteered to sacrifice himself to the monster's rage.

One day, Yseult said to Harold, "Will you go with me tomorrow evening to the feast in the sacred grove?"

"That I cannot do," answered Harold. "I have been summoned to Normandy on business. Swear that you will not go to the feast in the sacred grove without me."

"What do you say?" cried Yseult. "Shall I not go to the feast of Saint Alfreda? My father would be displeased if I were not there with the other maidens."

"Do not go, I beseech you," Harold pleaded. "If you love me, go not to the sacred grove! See—on my two knees I beg you!"

"How pale you are," said Yseult. "You are trembling!"

"Go not to the sacred grove tomorrow night," he begged.

Yseult was astonished. "From the way you speak," she said, "I might think you fear the werewolf. And by the cruel light in your eyes, one might almost take you to *be* the

Go SEARCH and KILL'...... and LO,

werewolf!"

Then Harold answered, "It is the werewolf that I fear. Come here, sit beside me. I will tell you why I fear for you. I dreamed that I was the werewolf. Do not shudder, dear love, for it was only a dream.

"In my dream, a gray and evil old man stood at my bedside and wanted to pluck my soul from my bosom. '*Your soul is mine,*' he said, '*You shall live out my curse. Give me your soul, I say.*'

"'What have I done that your curse should rest upon me?' I cried. 'You shall not have my soul.'

"'*For my wrongs shall you suffer: It is decreed.*'

"So spoke the old man. He plucked my soul from my bosom, Yseult, and he said, '*Go, search and kill*' — and lo, I was a wolf upon the moor!

"The dry grass crackled beneath my paws. The darkness of the night was

A A ARRGH !

s a WOLF upon the moor . . . .

heavy. Strange horrors tortured my soul, trapped in that wolfish body. The wind, in its many voices, whispered to me, saying, *'Go, search and kill.'* And above these voices sounded the hideous laughter of the old man.

"A forest lay before me with its gloomy thickets and its somber shadows. I saw its ravens, its vampires, its serpents, its reptiles, and all the terrible creatures of the night. The hares and other beasts sprang from my path. The curse was on me—I was the werewolf. I ran.

"On, on I went, with the fleetness of the wind. Nowhere was there pity for the wolf. The curse was on me and it filled me with a thirst for blood. 'Let me have human blood, that this curse may be removed,' I thought.

"At last I came to the sacred grove. Before me stood the old man. All other living things fled from me, but he feared me not. A maiden stood beside him. She did not see me, for she was blind.

"'*Kill, kill!*' cried the old man, and he pointed at the girl beside him.

"I sprang at her throat. I heard the old man's laughter once more, and then—then I awoke, shaking, cold, horrified."

Yseult trembled and stared into Harold's eyes. Then she whispered, "What a dark and evil dream. Dear Harold, what could it mean?"

Before Harold could reply, Alfred came by. Yseult told him that Harold was going away and how Harold had asked her not to attend the feast for fear of the werewolf.

"These fears are childish!" cried Alfred boastfully. "I will accompany you to the feast, and twenty of my best bowmen shall attend me. No werewolf will take a chance with us."

Harold went back to his home and fetched old Siegfried's spear. He handed it to Yseult, saying, "Take this spear with you to the feast. It will protect you." Then he hugged her and said, "Farewell, oh, my beloved. Farewell, farewell, forever." And so Harold went away, and Yseult worried over his strange behavior.

The next evening, Yseult went to the feast in the sacred grove. Tucked into her belt was old Siegfried's spear. Alfred accompanied her, along with twenty archers. In the grove there was great merriment. The folk celebrated the feast of Saint Alfreda with singing and dancing and games.

But suddenly a mighty uproar arose, and there were cries of "The werewolf! The werewolf!" Terror seized everyone. Out of the forest rushed the werewolf, gnashing his fangs and tossing yellow foam from his snapping jaws.

He headed straight for Yseult, as if an evil power drew him to her. But

10

Yseult was not afraid. Like a marble statue she stood and watched the werewolf coming. The archers, dropping their bows, fled. Alfred alone remained to battle the monster.

Alfred hurled his heavy lance at the approaching wolf. But as it struck the werewolf's bristling back, its point merely bent and it landed harmlessly.

Thinking of Harold's words, Yseult pulled old Siegfried's spear from her belt, raised it high, and with the strength of despair sent it hurtling through the air.

The werewolf saw the shining weapon, and a cry burst from his gaping throat. It was a cry of human agony. For an instant, Yseult saw in the werewolf's eyes the eyes of someone she had known. But then the eyes were no longer human, but wolfish in their ferocity.

A supernatural force seemed to speed the spear in its flight. With fearful precision the weapon buried itself deep in the werewolf's shaggy breast, just above the heart. With a monstrous sigh—as if he gave up his life without regret—the werewolf fell dead.

Then there was great joy, and loud were the cheers. Yseult was led home, where the people were preparing a great feast in her honor. The werewolf was dead, and Yseult had slain him.

But Yseult cried out: "Go, search for Harold. Go bring him to me."

"My lady," said Alfred, "how can we, since he has gone to Normandy?"

"I care not where he is!" she cried. "My heart stands still until I look into his eyes again."

"Surely he has not gone to Normandy," remarked a servant. "This very evening I saw him enter his home."

They rushed there. The door was locked.

"Harold, Harold, come out!" they cried, as they beat upon the door. But no answer came. Afraid, they battered down the door. When it fell, they saw Harold lying on his bed.

"He sleeps," said the servant. "See, he holds Yseult's portrait in his hand. How handsome and peaceful he looks."

But Harold was not asleep. His face was calm and beautiful, as if he was dreaming of his beloved. But his clothes were red with blood from a wound in his breast — a ghastly spear wound just above his heart.

KENNETH MORRIS

THE EYELESS DRAGONS

THE COURTYARD OF the Temple of Peace and Joy had been full since dawn. Everyone in the city of Nanking had been gossiping since the emperor announced he wanted a dragon painted on each of the two vast walls of the temple. When it was reported that Chang Seng-yu was to be the artist, then, indeed, the rejoicing was great.

The grand strokes of his brush were famous, and his colors were as delicate as evening mists on the Yangtse River, or as clear and lovely as the colors of flowers. Whenever he painted in public, crowds gathered to applaud his flashes of daring imagination.

Besides his genius with the brush, the crowds loved Chang Seng-yu for another reason. Many believed he had a magical gift. They believed that he could call the flying dragon and ride it to the ends of the earth. Some fourteen centuries ago, such things were done. One could never tell what might happen with any picture Chang Seng-yu was painting.

A hush settled over the temple court as the artist and his disciple

14

arrived, bearing brushes and pots of color. Chang Seng-yu was a quiet, gentle old man who bowed courteously to the crowd. For those who watched, painting was poetry made visible. It was Magic, the topmost wonder and delight of life.

Day by day the crowds gathered in the court and followed Chang Seng-yu into the vast temple. Day by day the silence was broken by murmurs and rippling applause. A sweep of Chang Seng-yu's brush, and lo, the jaws of a dragon appeared. Scale by scale, the wonderful windings of the vast body grew. It gleamed in shining yellow to the very end of the tail. Its elegant curves and noble lines graced the great wall. To behold it was like hearing the sudden crash of glorious and awe-inspiring music.

The crowd expected at any moment to see the dragon quiver, writhe, and shake itself loose from the wall. A little fear mingled with their intense delight. The Master was surely dealing in Magic.

"Sir," said Lu Chao, the Master's assistant, "for what reason have you not painted in the eye?"

"If this sacred dragon could see," answered Chang Seng-yu, "nothing could keep it from seeking its home in the sky."

15

"How is it possible?" said Lu Chao. "The dragon is beautiful, but it is only made of paint. How could it soar into the heavens?"

"Not so, Lu Chao," said the Master. "You have little understanding, as yet, of the mysteries of art."

But Lu Chao doubted, and it was a sorrow to him that Chang Seng-yu should leave his creation incomplete.

The Yellow Dragon was soon finished, its glorious form covering the upper part of the south wall. The people saw in it divine power, the perfect symbol of inspiration. "If the Master had not left his creation eyeless," they said, "the dragon would never be content to dwell on earth. The heavens are the right place for such a creature."

But Lu Chao went on doubting, and a shadow passed over Chang Seng-yu's face. "Lu Chao will never be a painter," he thought, sighing.

The scaffolding was taken to the opposite wall, and there, facing the other, the Purple Dragon began to grow. Occasionally, the emperor himself would visit the temple to inspect the work. He was impressed and honored. "But for what reason has the Master left the eyes to be painted last?" he asked.

"Sire," said Chang Seng-yu, "the eyes of the dragons will not be painted. There is danger that the dragons would not be contented with the earth, if they could see to soar into their rightful place among the heavens. Without their eyes, the dragons are content to remain here."

"It is good," said the emperor. "Let them remain to be the guardians of the temple of my people."

Lu Chao heard, but even the emperor's belief failed to convince him. "How could mere pictures feel a desire to soar to the heavens?" The work was drawing to a close, and Lu Chao doubted more and more.

Finally, the great work was completed. Priests, doctors, and all manner of important people gathered from neighboring kingdoms to witness the unveiling. All day long there were ceremonies and parades in the Temple of Peace and Joy. At last night came, and the great hall and courts were silent.

The time had come for Lu Chao. Now he would prove that the Master had been mistaken—that painted images could not shake themselves free from the walls. "It may be that there is Magic," said he, "but I have never seen it. Reason forbids me to believe in it."

He took a lantern, a small brush, and a jar of paint, and went down through the dark streets toward the temple. He met no one on the way.

He climbed the gate, found a ladder in the court, and placed it against

the south wall, by the head of the Yellow Dragon. He climbed up and prepared to paint the eye.

It had been a dark night, but calm. But as Lu Chao dipped the brush into the paint, there was a lightning flash and a peal of thunder. Its suddenness startled him. Were the spirits offended? He hesitated, and had some thought of going home. "But no," he said, "this is fear. This is superstition."

The lantern, hung from a rung close to the dragon's head, threw a little disk of brightness that lit the dragon's face. It was enough for Lu Chao's purpose. A few brush-strokes: that would be all.

With the first stroke, he felt fear. With the second, the wall seemed to become unsteady. And with the third, the sweat broke from his forehead and back. His hand began trembling violently. He gathered his mind, reasoning with himself. He steadied his hand and put in the last stroke. The Yellow Dragon's eye was painted.

Lu Chao clung to the ladder. By the small light of the lantern he saw the wonderful head turn until it was looking out into the temple, full face instead of profile. He had painted the left eye, but now two were there, glancing out proudly, uneasily. They flashed fiery rays through the empty darkness.

The ladder was shaking, swaying. Suddenly the two amazing eyes turned full on Lu Chao. A shadow of disgust flitted over them. Then they were filled with sadness and unbearable sorrow.

By the supernatural light from those eyes, Lu Chao saw the dragon draw its neck clear out of the wall. A crash, and he saw the immense wings shake forth. A horrible swaying of the world. A tearing and crashing. A blinding flame....

The entire city was awake and out in the streets. The people saw a golden wonder soaring up into the sky—a cometlike glory rising till it was lost in the darkness of heaven.

In the morning, the emperor visited the ruins of the Temple of Peace and Joy. With him was Chang Seng-yu, the Master. The roof had gone up in a blaze where the dragon's fiery wings had struck it. The north wall alone was standing. The rest had fallen. Under the debris they found the ladder, charred and broken, and the crushed body of Lu Chao.

"Ah," said Chang Seng-yu sadly, "I knew he would never have made an artist."

MOXON'S MASTER

AMBROSE BIERCE

"**A**RE YOU SERIOUS? Do you really believe that a machine can think?"

    I got no immediate reply. My friend Moxon was staring at the coals in the fireplace, touching them with the poker till they glowed. It was easy to see that he had something on his mind.

    Finally he said: "I used to think the answer was 'no.' If you build something, how can it be alive?"

    He rose abruptly and looked out of a window into the blackness of the stormy night. A moment later he turned around and said: "Now I believe differently. I believe that a machine thinks about the work that it is doing."

His response troubled me. Moxon's devotion to his machines had not been good for him. Had it affected his mind? His surprising reply to my question seemed to be evidence that it had.

"And what does it think with, since it has no brain?" I asked.

But before Moxon could respond, we were interrupted by a sound coming from his machine shop. It was private, and he hardly allowed anyone to enter it. From within came a thumping sound, as of someone pounding upon a table with an open hand.

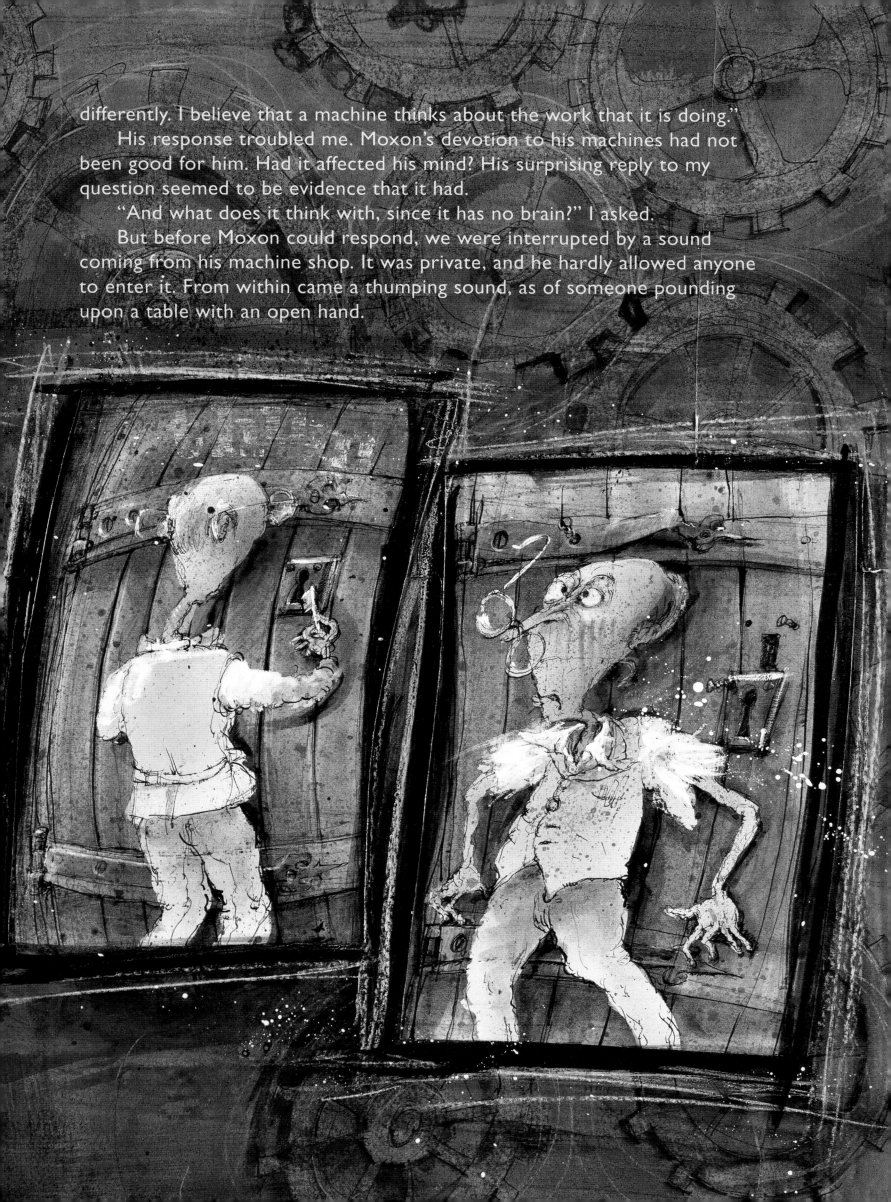

Moxon, visibly disturbed, rose and hurried into the machine shop. I thought it odd that anyone would be in there. There were confused sounds, and the floor shook. Then all was silent, and soon Moxon reappeared and said, with a rather sorry smile:

"Pardon me for leaving you so abruptly. I have a machine in there that lost its temper."

I stared at his left cheek, which bore four long, bloody scratches.

"You should trim its nails," I said.

Moxon paid no attention to my joke. He sat down and was silent for a long time, gazing absently into the fire. It was growing late, but I did not like the notion of leaving him in that isolated house, all alone with some unknown person who might be dangerous.

I leaned toward him and said: "Moxon, who is in there?"

Somewhat to my surprise he laughed lightly and answered without hesitation: "Nobody. The trouble was that I left a machine with nothing for it to work on."

"I'm going to wish you a good night," I said, rising and taking my overcoat. "And I hope that machine will have its gloves on the next time you want to stop it."

Without waiting to observe the effect of my wisecrack, I left the house.

Rain was falling, and the darkness was intense. In the sky beyond the crest of a hill I could see the faint glow of the city's lights. Behind me nothing was visible but a single window of Moxon's house. I knew it was an uncurtained window in my friend's machine shop. I had little doubt that he had resumed his work in that mysterious room.

As I walked, my mind played over Moxon's idea that machines can think. It was an odd belief, but it was also fascinating. I had to hear more. Without thinking, I turned around, and almost before I was aware of it, I found myself again at Moxon's door.

I was drenched with rain. Entering, I mounted the stairs to the room that I had so recently left. All was dark and silent. Moxon, as I had supposed, was in the machine shop. I groped along the wall until I found the door. I knocked loudly several times, but got no response. The uproar outside probably prevented me from being heard. The wind was blowing hard and dashing the rain against the thin walls.

I had never been invited into the machine shop. No one was allowed in—

except for a skilled metalworker. No one knew anything about him except that his name was Haley and that he kept silent. But in my excited state of mind I cracked open the door. What I saw proved to me that Moxon knew what he was talking about.

Moxon sat facing me at the far side of a small table. Upon the table, a single candle made all the light that was in the room. Opposite him, his back toward me, sat another person. Between the two was a chessboard. The men were playing. There were only a few pieces left on the board. It was obvious that the game was near its end.

Moxon was concentrating hard—not so much on the game as on his opponent. Moxon's gaze was so intense that he didn't notice me at all. Moxon's face was ghastly white and his eyes glittered like diamonds. I had only a back view of his opponent, but that was enough. I did not want to see his face.

He was apparently not more than five feet in height. With his tremendously wide shoulders and thick, short neck, the figure reminded me of a gorilla. His broad, squat head, which had a tangled growth of black hair, was topped with a crimson fez. A tunic of the same color, belted tightly at the waist, reached the seat—apparently a box—upon which he sat. I could not see his legs. He moved his pieces with his right hand, which seemed unusually long.

The play was rapid. Moxon hardly glanced at the board before making his moves. His motions were quick and nervous. The response of his opponent was a slow, uniform, mechanical movement of the right arm. There was something unearthly about it all, and I caught myself shuddering.

Two or three times after moving a piece the stranger slightly inclined his head, and each time I observed that Moxon shifted his king. All at once the thought came to me that the stranger was a machine—a robot chess player!

So this was why Moxon was so interested in

whether machines could think! I was about to leave when something strange happened.

I observed a shrug of the robot's great shoulders, as if it were irritated. It was so natural—so entirely human—that it startled me. That was not all, for a moment later it struck the table sharply with its clenched hand. Moxon seemed even more startled than I was. He pushed his chair backward a little in alarm.

It was Moxon's turn. After a few moments, he raised his hand high above the board and pounced upon one of the pieces like a hawk. Exclaiming "Checkmate! I win!" he rose quickly to his feet and stepped behind his chair. The robot sat motionless.

The wind had now gone down, but I heard, at lessening intervals and progressively louder, the rumble and roll of thunder. In the pauses between I became aware of a low humming or buzzing which, like the thunder, grew louder. It seemed to come from the body of the robot.

It was unmistakably a whirring of gears. It gave me the impression of a machine that has begun to go out of control. But before I had much time to think about it, the robot began making strange motions.

A slight but continuous shudder took it over. Its body and head shook like a man with a chill. The motion grew stronger every moment until the entire figure was rocking violently.

Suddenly it sprang to its feet. With a movement almost too quick for the eye to follow, it shot across the table, with both arms thrust forward to their full length.

Moxon tried to throw himself backward out of reach, but he was too late. I saw the horrible thing's hands close upon Moxon's throat. Moxon clutched the thing's wrists. Then the table was overturned, and the candle was thrown to the floor and extinguished. Everything was dark. But the noise of the struggle was dreadful, and most terrible of all were the squawking sounds Moxon made as he tried to breathe.

I sprang to the rescue of my friend, but had hardly taken a stride in the darkness when the whole room blazed with a blinding white light. It burned into my memory a vivid picture of the combatants on the floor. Moxon was underneath, his throat still in the clutch of those iron hands, his head forced backward, his mouth wide open, and his eyes wide with terror.

In horrible contrast was the painted face of the thing. It wore an expression of tranquil and profound thought, as if it had found the solution to a chess problem! This I saw, then all was blackness and silence.

Three days later I recovered consciousness in a hospital room. I recognized Moxon's confidential workman, Haley, who had come to visit me. He approached, smiling.

"Tell me about it," I managed to say, faintly—"all about it."

"Certainly," he said. "You were carried unconscious from Moxon's burning house. Nobody knows how you got there. The origin of the fire is a bit

mysterious, too. I think the house was struck by lightning."

"And Moxon?"

"Buried yesterday...what was left of him."

After some moments of pain I ventured to ask another question:

"Who rescued me?"

"Well, if that interests you—I did."

"Thank you, Mr. Haley, and
may God bless you for it.

Did you rescue, also, that product of your skill, the robot chess player that murdered its inventor?"

The man was silent a long time, looking away from me. Then he turned and gravely said:

"Are you sure it did that?"

"I do," I replied. "I saw it."

That was many years ago. If you ask me today, I can still hardly believe it.

'Twas brillig and the slithy toves
Did gyre and gimble in the wabe;
All mimsy were the borogoves,
And the mome raths outgrabe.

JABBERWOCKY LEWIS CARROLL

"Beware the Jabberwock, my son!
The jaws that BITE,
The CLAWS that CATCH!
Beware the JubJub bird,
And shun
The frumious
Bandersnatch!"

He took his VORPAL Sword in hand:
Longtime the manxome foe he sought—
So rested he by the Tumtum tree,
And stood awhile in thought.

And as in uffish thought he stood,
The JABBERWOCK, with eyes of FLAME,
Came whiffling through the tulgey wood,
And BURBLED as it CAME!

One, two! ONE, TWO! And through and through
The VORPAL blade went snicker-snack!
He left it DEAD, and with its HEAD
He went galumphing back.

"And hast thou SLAIN the JABBERWOCK?
Come to my arms, my beamish boy!
O frabjous day! Callooh! Callay!"
He chortled in his joy.

'Twas brillig, and the slithy toves
Did gyre and gimble in the wabe;
All mimsy were the borogoves,
And the mome raths outgrabe.

MARY WOLLSTONECRAFT SHELLEY

I AM THE CREATURE that Dr. Frankenstein created. He has given me life, but now we are enemies. I know he means to destroy me.

I have no name. Some call me Frankenstein, after my creator. Those who have seen me call me the Monster. How can I make them understand that I am not one?

Dr. Victor Frankenstein is a gifted scientist. His goal was to eliminate death. In his experiments, he found the secret of bringing dead matter back to life. I am the result. To Dr. Frankenstein, I am a grotesque horror sewn together from lifeless scraps. To him I am an experiment gone wrong. But I am alive! I have the power of thought. I have emotions—and yes—I can speak. But who will listen to me when even my creator has turned his back on my hideous appearance?

How did he feel as he worked into the night, stealing fresh corpses from the morgue? As he was stitching me together in his secret laboratory, was he proud and hopeful? Did he think about what his creature would be like? To make the surgery easier, the doctor made me of gigantic size. Did it occur to him that he was also magnifying my talent for causing terror?

However noble the doctor's intentions, he has never shown me anything but hatred and disgust. As I lay on the slab in his laboratory, electricity tingled through my veins, filling me with the life force. I felt Frankenstein's presence even before I could open my eyes. When my eyes did open, the first thing I saw was the doctor standing over me. His face wore a look of agony. From the beginning it was clear to me—Dr. Frankenstein dreaded his experiment.

When he saw that I was alive, Frankenstein fled the laboratory, leaving me alone. No doubt he hoped I would die. But the doctor did his work well. I am stronger and more agile than any natural man. Where the doctor failed was in my appearance. I am ugly beyond words, and this is my curse.

I escaped the laboratory shortly after, and went into the night. I thought the world was incredibly beautiful—the stars twinkled in the heavens, the silver orb of the moon beamed its friendly light, the crickets sang. I found shelter that night in

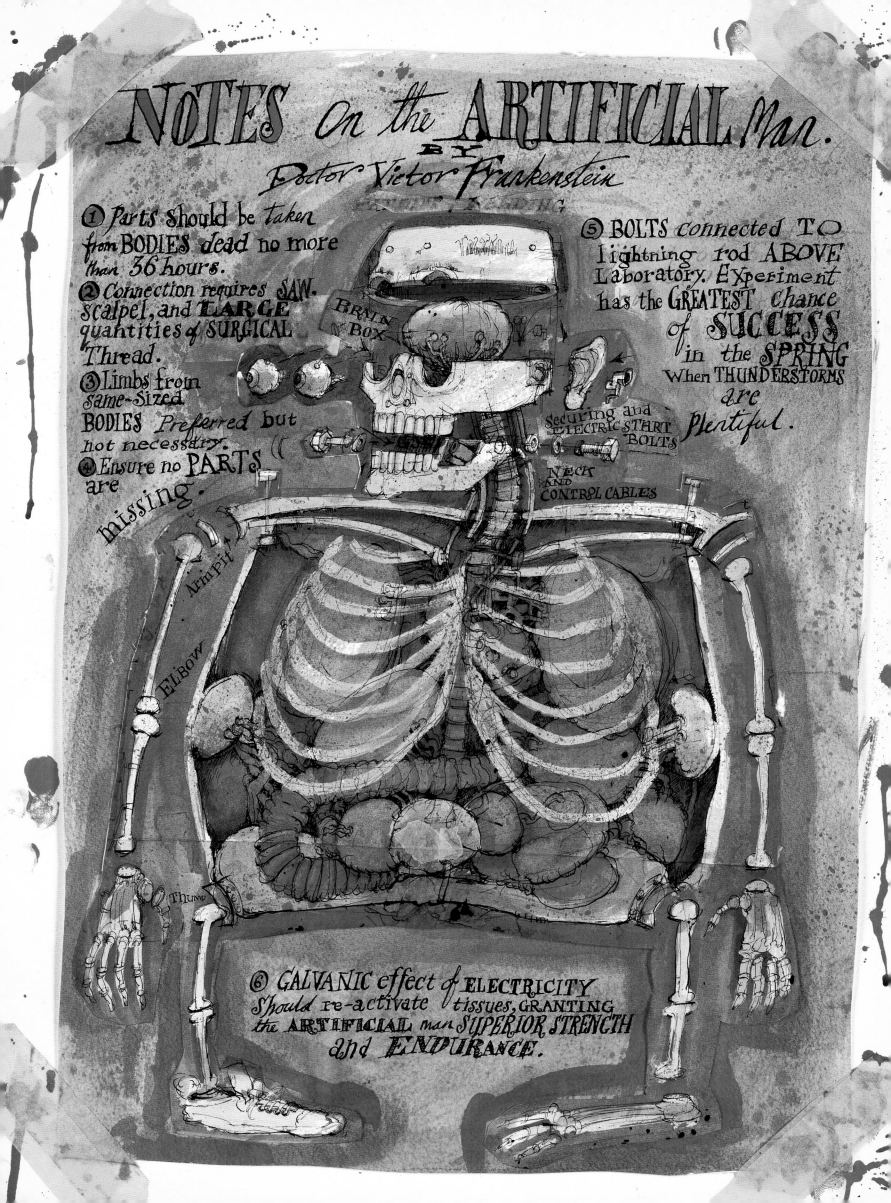

the fragrant, mossy woods.

The morning brought with it greater wonders—a golden sunrise, gentle warmth, the graceful flight and beautiful sounds of the birds. How good to be alive!

My joy would soon be ruined. As I approached the village, people screamed and threw stones. They ran to their homes and bolted the doors and windows.

Once I came upon a cottage with a small shed attached. When it was dark, I moved into the shed and made a home there. Through a crack in the wall, I could peer into the cottage. An old, blind man lived there with his son and young daughter. For months I stayed hidden in the shed, leaving only late at night. By watching and listening through the crack, I received the gift of language.

Even though I did not dare try to meet them, and they did not know I existed, I grew to love this family. They were poor and hard-working, but how I envied their life and their happiness! To help them with their work, I gathered wood at night and piled it near their house. They believed they were being helped by a spirit of the forest. It warmed my heart to help lessen their burden.

Finally, I felt I must meet these kind people. I drew in my mind a thousand pictures of how I might present myself to them. At first they would be disgusted by my appearance, but through gentle words I could surely win their trust.

I thought I could befriend the old man first. Since he could not see me, he would not be afraid of me. My chance came when the boy and girl went off together, leaving the old man by himself.

Summoning all my courage, I knocked on the cottage door. The old man welcomed me inside. I explained that I was a traveler, going to meet my friends, and I asked to rest for a spell. We talked warmly. The old man was kind and patient.

Suddenly the door opened. The others had returned! The girl screamed. I grabbed the old man's hand. "Please, sir, protect me! I mean no harm," I cried.

The young man, with surprising force, pulled his father from me. He knocked me to the ground and hit me violently with a stick. Overcome with pain and anguish, I ran from the cottage and into the woods. When I dared to approach the cottage again,

two days later, I found it abandoned.

Alone once more, I searched for a companion and for a place where I might fit in. One stormy night, desperation led me back to the home of my creator. I watched him through the window of his study. I knew I would not be welcome. I watched for almost an hour, hidden in the darkness. Then a bolt of lightning struck a nearby tree, creating a terrible crash and lighting the sky. The doctor turned to the window, and there he saw me against the glass. His fright was deep. I pushed the window open and entered the room.

"Hideous monster!" shouted the doctor. "Begone! You have no business here!"

"But we do have business, Doctor," I said. "You have created me and then cruelly cast me out. The world has shown me no favor. I know my visit brings you misery, but I too am miserable. If you will lessen my pain, I swear that you will never see me again."

"What is it you ask of me, creature?" spat the doctor.

"You must create a female for me, whom I can love and who will love me. If you create for me a companion as deformed as I am, I will find peace."

"I refuse, monster, and no torture shall ever force me to agree. My only obligation is to mankind, not to you. And that duty is to destroy you."

Rage and disappointment burned within me. I fled through the open window and into the night.

To this day I wander, over mountains, across the sea, to the remote and icy caps of the earth. I search only for a friend.

HOW BEOWULF defeated GRENDEL

ANONYMOUS

MIGHTY KING HROTHGAR of the Danes did not know what to do. For his warriors, he had built a great feasting hall. But the hall had seen little joy. A savage and cruel demon known as Grendel had risen from the misty swamps. Coming in the night, Grendel had killed thirty soldiers. Weapons were useless against him. He couldn't be bribed with gold. All Grendel wanted was human flesh.

Word of Hrothgar's problem reached Beowulf, a brave warrior of the Geat nation. Beowulf was the strongest and noblest of all men. Gathering other gallant soldiers, he sailed to the land of the Danes.

As Beowulf's ship drew close to the Danish shore, sunlight glinted off the polished shields his men carried. One of Hrothgar's guards, looking out to sea, saw the armor of these visitors and was alarmed. With his spear in hand, he spurred his horse and met the ship as it reached the beach.

"Who are you, that you come bearing weapons to this land?" challenged the sentry. "I have guarded this land for many years and never have I seen such a mighty warrior as you," he said to Beowulf. "Where do you come from, and what is your mission?"

"I am Beowulf, the son of Ecgtheow," said Beowulf. "He was a man known to all, and a

good friend of your king, Hrothgar. I am here to rid your land of the monster Grendel."

"It will be no easy task," said the astonished guard. "But if any man can destroy the evil Grendel, he would be you. Come, let me present you to the king. He will be pleased to see you."

Brave-hearted Beowulf marched to the hall with his warriors and was brought before Hrothgar. Beowulf's armor and helmet gleamed like none anyone had ever seen.

"Good Beowulf," said Hrothgar, "your father was a great man and a true friend. When we last met, you were just a boy. Now you have grown to be as mighty as your father. What brings you over the sea to the land of the Danes?"

Beowulf spoke: "Hail Hrothgar! The horrors of Grendel became known to me. I have come to settle affairs with this monster. I am as strong as Grendel," swore Beowulf, "and I will use no weapons against him. We will fight hand to hand."

"Others have sworn to destroy Grendel," replied Hrothgar, "and they have not lived to see the next day. But you are a man above men. I can see that you will be Grendel's destroyer. Let us have a feast to celebrate your arrival."

That night the great hall, which had been empty for so long, rang with merriment. After the feast, Beowulf and the warriors lay down to sleep. They all knew that somewhere, the monster waited.

In the dead of night, Grendel rose from the swamp. He came gliding through the moors to the hall. One swipe of his mighty claw smashed open the door. In a moment he was inside. His eyes burned like flames as he spied the sleeping soldiers. His heart laughed as he thought about ripping apart each and every warrior.

In no time he grabbed a sleeping soldier, tore him to shreds, and crunched his bones. The other warriors grabbed their shields and swords. But their weapons could not pierce Grendel's skin, and they were swept aside like toys.

Grendel strode to Beowulf's bed and reached toward him. Beowulf sat up and grabbed the monster's arm first. He held on until his fingers cracked. Grendel was alarmed. No one had ever treated him like this! He tried to pull away, but Beowulf would not let go. His strength was incredible. The courageous soldier pulled harder as the horrible creature screamed and struggled.

Together, Beowulf and Grendel crashed about the great hall. Both were enraged. They knocked over the heavy tables, and the floor shook. Grendel could not shake free from Beowulf's mighty grip. Then, screaming in agony, Grendel felt his arm slip out of its socket.

The monster bellowed horribly, and everyone heard the sound of ripping flesh. Then suddenly—a snap. Beowulf had torn off Grendel's arm!

In unbearable pain, Grendel fled from the hall. He crawled back into the steaming moors to die.

Grendel was dead! The terror was over! Now King Hrothgar and his people could rejoice. The hall was repaired and hung with golden tapestries. Grendel's fearsome severed arm was hung on the wall as a trophy.

A great banquet was prepared, and Beowulf was the guest of honor. The hall was filled with happy noise. The queen gave Beowulf treasure, including armor made of precious metals, a jeweled saddle, and a gold necklace. Beowulf nobly accepted the gifts and swore his friendship to the king.

"Not long ago, I thought I would never live to see this day," said Hrothgar. "Beowulf, you are the best of men, and I love you like a son. Wear this necklace well, and may it bring you luck. May all men praise you, far and near. Long may you live, and vast be your treasure."

Thus did the king salute Beowulf, and peace reigned over the land of the Danes.

The MAN-EATING tree

PHIL ROBINSON

MY GREAT-UNCLE WAS a great traveler. The tales he told of his adventures were always fascinating and bizarre, but they were all absolutely true. His most astounding story was about a man-eating tree.

"Many years ago," said my uncle, "I turned my restless steps toward Central Africa, which at that time was unexplored and dangerous. With me was Otona, a young lad from the uplands who was my guide. After setting up our tent one day, Otona and I found we were low on food. We decided to go hunting in a nearby fern forest.

"As we approached the forest, we found it was cut into two by a clearing. A group of small antelope browsed their way along the shaded side. The herd was suspicious and slowly trotted along before us. Creeping along, we followed them along the edge of the fern growths. Turning a corner I suddenly became aware of a single tree growing in the middle of the glade—one tree alone. It struck me that I had never seen a tree exactly like

it before.

"The deer were midway between me and the tree. I fired my rifle into the middle of the herd. I hit one. The rest of the herd ran off in the direction of the tree. The wounded one was left behind. Otona ran to catch it, but the little creature, seeing him coming, tried to follow the others. The herd had meanwhile reached the tree. Suddenly, instead of passing under it, they swept around it at a distance.

"Was I crazy? Or did the plant really try to catch the deer? Suddenly I saw, or thought I saw, the tree violently waving. While the ferns all around stood motionless in the dead evening air, the tree's boughs swayed toward the herd. I closed my eyes for a moment and looked again. The tree was motionless.

"Otona was running after the deer. He stretched out his hands to catch it. It bounded from his grasp. Again he reached forward, and again it escaped him. Another rush forward, and the next instant both boy and deer were beneath the tree.

"And now there was no mistaking what I saw.

"The tree was in motion. It leaned forward, swept its thick leafy boughs to the ground, and grabbed Otona and the deer! Otona's cry came to me in all its agony. There was then one strangling scream, and except for the shaking of the leaves, there was not a sign of life!

"I called out 'Otona!' No answer came. I tried to call out again, but my voice was frozen. Not all the terrors of earth could have made me take my foot off the ground. But my reason slowly returned. Perhaps Otona had fallen into the lair of some beast, I thought. Preparing to defend myself, I approached the silent tree. But

"Above me I SAW a GREAT LIMB....?

the terrible truth could not be denied.

"The tree first noticed me when I was about fifty yards away. The motion among the thick-lipped leaves reminded me of a vast pit full of snakes.

"I came within twenty yards of it. The tree was quivering through every branch, yearning towards me. Each leaf was agitated and hungry. Like fleshy lips or tongues they fumbled together, closing on each other and falling open again. Each was dimpled with little cup-like hollows.

"I approached nearer and nearer, step by step. I was now within ten yards of the farthest reaching bough. Every part of the tree was hysterical with excitement. The motion was awful—sickening yet fascinating. In their eagerness for the food so near them, the leaves turned upon each other. Two would suck together face to face and writhe like some green worm. Then at last they would slowly separate.

"One large leaf, vampire-like, had sucked the juices out of a smaller one. A sticky dew glistened in the dimples, welled over, and trickled down each leaf. The sound of it dripping from leaf to leaf made it seem as if the tree was muttering to itself.

"Above me I saw a great limb. Every one of its thousand clammy lips reached downwards towards me, fumbling. It strained, shivered, rocked, and heaved. The boughs tossed to this side and to that, tantalized by my presence. I felt the vile dew fall upon me.

"Then, leaning over, I saw the many-lipped monster slowly pulling up its roots from the softened ground. It was moving toward me!

"I fired my gun at the approaching horror. The shot tore into the soft body of the great thing. The trunk shuddered. Then I saw a large branch slowly droop, and without a sound it broke off the trunk.

"I fired again, and another vile branch was dead. Each shot killed more of the plant. And so I attacked it, killing a leaf here and a branch there. When my ammunition was gone, the giant was a wreck—as if some hurri-

43

cane had torn through it. On the ground lay the fragments, struggling, rising and falling, gasping.

"I had drawn my hunting knife, and was fighting—*with the leaves.* Each leaf had a life of its own. More than once I felt my hand seized as if by sharp teeth. I rushed forward over the fallen foliage, and with my last bit of strength I drove my knife into the soft trunk. Pulling myself out of the thickening sap, I dragged myself back to the tent, where I fell, exhausted and unconscious.

"It was the next day before I could approach the terrible thing. When I went back, it was quite dead. I removed the rotting leaves, and there, at the roots, was the ghastly corpse of Otona. To have removed the leaves would have taken too long, so I buried the body as it was—with a hundred vampire leaves still clinging to it."

Such, as nearly as I remember it, was my great-uncle's story of the man-eating tree.

BANG BANG BANG!

CHARLES DICKENS

In an old abbey town, many years ago, there was a sexton named Gabriel Grub. Gabriel was a surly, gloomy, and lonely man. He greeted everyone with a deep scowl of malice. It was difficult to pass Gabriel Grub without feeling worse afterward.

A little before twilight one Christmas Eve, Gabriel lighted his lantern, shouldered his spade, and went to the old churchyard. As sexton, it was his job to dig graves. He was feeling very low, and thought that digging a grave might lift his spirits.

As he wound his way through the ancient streets, he saw the cheerful light of blazing fires gleam through the old windows. He heard the loud laughs and the cheerful shouts of the people around them. He noted the bustling preparations for the next day's celebrations.

All this was fuss and bother to Gabriel Grub. He strode through the light snow, returning the good-humored greetings of his neighbors with a short, sullen growl.

Gabriel turned into the dark lane which led to the churchyard. He had been looking forward to reaching the dark lane, because it was a nice, gloomy place. Gabriel was a little annoyed to hear a young boy singing out some jolly song about a merry Christmas.

Gabriel waited till the boy came up. Then he chased the boy into a corner and rapped him over the head with his lantern five or six times, just to teach him to control his voice. And as the boy hurried away with his hands on his head, Gabriel Grub chuckled very heartily to himself. He entered the churchyard and locked the gate behind him.

He set down his lantern, took off his coat, and getting into the unfinished grave, worked at it for an hour or so. When he had nearly finished work for the night, Gabriel Grub sat himself down on a flat tombstone, which was a favorite resting place of his.

"Ho! Ho!" he laughed. "A coffin at Christmas—a Christmas Box. Ho! Ho! Ho!"

"Ho! Ho! Ho!" repeated a voice close behind him.

Gabriel looked around in some alarm. The snow lay hard and crisp upon the ground, and spread over the thickly-strewn mounds of earth. All was cold and still in the pale moonlight.

"It was an echo," said Gabriel Grub.

"It was not," said a deep voice.

Gabriel sprang up and stood rooted to the spot with astonishment and terror. His eyes rested on a form which made his blood run cold.

Seated nearby, on an upright tombstone, was a strange, unearthly figure. Gabriel knew at once it was no being of this world. His long, fantastic legs were cocked up and crossed. His sinewy arms were bare, and his hands rested on his knees. On his short, round body he wore a close covering, ornamented with small slashes. A short cloak dangled at his back. The collar was cut into curious peaks. His shoes curled up at the toes into long points. On his head he wore a broad-brimmed hat garnished with a single feather. The hat was covered with white frost.

The goblin looked as if he had sat on the same tombstone, very comfortably, for two or three hundred years. He was sitting perfectly still, sticking out his tongue and grinning at Gabriel Grub with such a grin as only a goblin could call up.

Gabriel Grub was paralyzed, and could make no reply.

"What are you doing here on Christmas Eve?" said the goblin sternly.

"I—I came to dig a grave, sir," stammered Gabriel Grub.

"What man wanders among graves and churchyards on such a night as this?" said the goblin.

"Gabriel Grub! Gabriel Grub!" screamed a wild chorus of voices that seemed to fill the churchyard. Gabriel looked fearfully around—nothing was to be seen.

The goblin leered maliciously at the terrified sexton, and then raising his voice, exclaimed:

"And who, then, is our fair and lawful prize?"

To this question the invisible chorus sang to the mighty swell of the old

church organ, "Gabriel Grub! Gabriel Grub!"

The sexton gasped for breath.

"What do you think of this, Gabriel?" said the goblin, kicking up his feet and looking at the turned-up points of his shoes.

"It's—it's very strange, sir," replied the sexton, half dead with fright. "Very strange, but I think I'll go back and finish my work, sir, if you please."

"Work!" said the goblin. "What work?"

"The grave, sir, making the grave," stammered the sexton.

"Oh, the grave, eh?" said the goblin. "Who makes graves at a time when all other men are merry, and takes pleasure in it?"

Again the mysterious voices replied, "Gabriel Grub! Gabriel Grub!"

"I'm afraid my friends want you, Gabriel," said the goblin.

"I don't think the gentlemen know me, sir," replied the horror-struck sexton.

"We know the man with the sulky face and the grim scowl that came down

the street tonight, throwing his evil looks at the children," answered the goblin. "We know the man that struck the boy because the boy could be merry, and he could not. We know him, we know him."

Here the goblin gave a loud, shrill laugh that the echoes returned twenty-fold. Throwing his legs up in the air, the goblin stood upon his head—or rather upon the very point of his hat—on the narrow edge of the tombstone. He threw a somersault right to the sexton's feet.

"I—I—am afraid I must leave you, sir," said the sexton.

"Leave us!" said the goblin, "Gabriel Grub going to leave us. Ho! Ho! Ho!"

As the goblin laughed, the church organ pealed forth a lively tune. Whole troops of goblins, very much like the first one, poured into the churchyard and began playing leapfrog with the tombstones. They never stopped for an instant to take a breath. The organ played quicker and quicker, and the goblins leaped faster and faster, coiling themselves up, rolling head over heels upon the ground,

and bounding over the tombstones like balls. The sexton's brain whirled as the spirits flew before his eyes. The first goblin suddenly darted towards him, laid his hand upon his collar, and sank with him through the earth.

When Gabriel Grub had had time to recover his breath, he found himself in a large cavern. He was surrounded on all sides by crowds of goblins, ugly and grim. In the center of the room, on an elevated seat, was the leader of the goblins from the churchyard. Gabriel Grub stood beside him, unable to move.

"Cold tonight," said the king of the goblins, "very cold. A glass of something warm, here."

At this command, a grinning goblin stepped forward with a goblet of liquid fire, which he presented to the king.

"Ah!" said the goblin king, whose cheeks and throat were quite transparent as he tossed down the flame, "this warms one, indeed. Bring a glass of the same for Mr. Grub."

It was in vain for the unfortunate sexton to protest. One of the goblins held him while another poured the blazing liquid down his throat. All the goblins screeched with laughter as he coughed and choked, and wiped away the tears from his eyes after swallowing the burning beverage.

"And now," said the king, poking his face into the sexton's — "and now, show the man of misery and gloom a few of the pictures from our great storehouse."

As the goblin said this, a thick cloud which covered the far end of the cavern rolled gradually away. It revealed a small and scantily furnished, but neat and clean apartment. A crowd of little children were gathered round a bright fire, clinging to their mother's gown, and playing round her chair. A frugal meal was spread upon the table. A knock was heard, and the children clapped their hands as their father entered.

The father was wet and weary. He shook the snow from his garments as the children crowded round him. Then as the father sat down to his meal before the fire, the children climbed about his knee. The mother sat by his side, and everyone seemed happy.

But a change came upon the view. The scene shifted to a small bedroom, where the fairest and youngest child lay dying. The color had fled from his cheeks, and the light from his eye. As the sexton looked upon him, the child died. His young brothers and sisters crowded round his little bed and seized his tiny hand, so cold and heavy. He seemed to be sleeping in rest and peace. They knew that he was an angel looking down upon them, blessing them from a bright and happy heaven.

Then they rose and turned away. But their cries were not bitter, for they knew that they should one day meet again. The cloud settled upon the picture and concealed it from the sexton's view.

"What do you think of that?" said the goblin, turning his large face toward

Gabriel Grub.

Gabriel answered that he didn't like the people, and that the boy's death was a pretty scene.

"You miserable man!" shouted the goblin. "You!" He seemed about to add more, but anger choked him. Instead he lifted up one of his legs and gave Gabriel Grub a good, sound kick in the behind. Then all the goblins crowded round the wretched sexton and kicked his bottom without mercy.

"Show him some more," said the king of the goblins.

At these words the cloud was again dispelled, and a rich and beautiful landscape was revealed. It was a bright, balmy summer morning. The sun shone in the clear blue sky. The trees rustled in the light wind that murmured among their leaves, and the birds sang upon the boughs. People strolled by, elated with the scene, in all its brightness and splendor.

"That," said the king of goblins, "is pretty." Again he kicked the sexton, and again the other goblins imitated his example.

Many a time the cloud went and came. Each time the scene changed, it taught Gabriel Grub a new lesson.

He saw that men who worked hard to earn their livings were cheerful and happy. He saw that the beauty of nature was a never-failing source of cheerfulness and joy. He saw that people who held happiness in their hearts could overcome the cruelest hardships and suffering.

Above all, he saw that men like himself, who snarled at the mirth and cheerfulness of others, were the foulest weeds on earth. When he compared all the good in the world with all the evil, he decided that it was a very decent and respectable sort of world after all. No sooner had he realized this than the cloud closed over the last picture. One by one the goblins faded from sight, and as the last one disappeared, Gabriel sunk into a deep sleep.

Day had broken when Gabriel Grub awoke. He found himself lying on the flat gravestone in the churchyard. His coat, spade, and lantern, all well-whitened by the last night's frost, lay scattered on the ground.

The stone on which he had first seen the goblin stood upright before him, and the grave at which he had worked the night before was not far off. At first he began to doubt the reality of his adventures. But the pain in his behind when he tried to rise assured him that the kicking of the goblins was certainly not imaginary.

Gabriel Grub got to his feet. Brushing the frost off his coat, he put it on and turned his face toward the town. But he was a changed man. He was happier, and more affectionate. He could not bear the thought of returning to a place where no one would believe his brighter attitude. He paused for a few moments, and then turned away to begin his life again.